FIC
WI

MW01066030

FRIENDS ON ICE

Sharla Scannell Whalen

Illustrations by Virginia Kylberg
Spot Illustrations by Helen Kunzi

ABDO & Daughters
Minneapolis

Published by Abdo & Daughters, 4940 Viking Drive, Suite 622, Edina, Minnesota 55435.

Printed in the United States.

Illustrations by Virginia Kylberg

Edited by Laura Vadaj and Ken Berg

Library of Congress Cataloging-in-Publication Data

Whalen, Sharla Scannell, 1960-
    Friends on ice / Sharla Scannell Whalen.
    p. cm.
    Summary: In the 1890s in Illinois, Beth is dismayed to find her friendship with Maggie in trouble as the Winter Entertainment approaches.
    ISBN 1-56239-901-2
    [1. Friendship--Fiction.] I. Title.
    PZ7.W5455Fr 1997
    [Fic]--dc21   97-2583
                                   CIP
                                   AC

Table of Contents

CHAPTER ONE
New Year's Blues   4

CHAPTER TWO
Buttons and Beaux   11

CHAPTER THREE
Stirring Up Memories   17

CHAPTER FOUR
Valentine Mystery   22

CHAPTER FIVE
Putting Two and Two Together   28

CHAPTER SIX
Bumps and Bruises   31

CHAPTER SEVEN
Hot Chocolate in an Octagon   38

CHAPTER EIGHT
Midnight Adventure   44

CHAPTER NINE
The Snow Princess   51

CHAPTER TEN
Blizzard on the Farm   57

CHAPTER
ONE

NEW YEAR'S BLUES

"Fractious" was the word Aunt Mary had used to describe Beth Dunstable at the breakfast table this morning. And now, looking out at the snowy town of Oakdale from her bedroom window, Beth Dunstable was irritable.

She tried to figure out just why she felt this way. "First of all," she thought, "the holidays are over, and there's nothing to look forward to."

"What else?" thought Beth. "All this snow, I suppose. Sometimes it makes me feel kind of cooped up." The Illinois prairie was having its coldest and snowiest winter in many years.

"On the other hand, it's wonderful skating weather." Beth's dog, Snowflake, pushed his white head against her. She scratched his ears absent-mindedly.

The thought of skating made Beth feel gloomy

again. The day before, she and her friends Maggie Sullivan, Ellie Perry, and Hannah Olson had met on the frozen river to skate. Beth and Maggie had quarreled.

Beth had received a new pair of skates for Christmas, even though her old skates weren't yet outgrown and still gleaming white. She was sure the old pair would fit Maggie and had brought them to the river. But Maggie had tossed her red curls and sniffed, "I don't want your nasty old castoffs, Beth Dunstable!"

"Old?" Beth had exclaimed. "These are practically brand-new."

"I never asked for them and I don't want them." Maggie had slung over her shoulder the old brown skates inherited from her brother Kevin and stomped away.

"The skates are hardly castoffs," Beth thought.

The truth was, she had seen an advertisement for a pair of stylish ice skates with pointed toes. They looked so grown-up, Beth felt she had to add them to her Christmas wish list. Why had she assumed that Maggie would like her old pair if they were too babyish for herself? Was that why Maggie was angry?

A soft knock sounded on Beth's bedroom door and

Agnes, the housekeeper, looked in. "I noticed you didn't eat much at breakfast, dear," she said. "I brought you up a little something."

Agnes' idea of "a little something" was usually a full meal. But this time she just brought in a silver tray with a pot of hot chocolate and a plate of gingerbread cookies. "Are you feeling well?"

"I'm fine," answered Beth morosely. Agnes wisely asked no further questions. She set the tray down on Beth's pink-skirted vanity table, smiled fondly, and closed the door quietly behind her.

But, even the treat of hot chocolate failed to cheer up Beth. So she turned back to the window.

A fresh blanket of snow made everything look mysterious on Jefferson street below. The forsythia bushes on the wide front lawn were big snowy lumps. Beth wondered if the high school boys were over at the river, shoveling it clear for the Sunday skaters.

"But I'm not going today," Beth thought. She was still feeling prickly.

§

Across the DuPage River, on the other side of town, Maggie was sitting in her family's small parlor, feeling as grumpy as Beth.

At the moment, however, Maggie was blaming her troubles on her little brother and sisters. Especially six-year-old Brigid, who was standing relentlessly at Maggie's elbow. She stood there despite the growling responses Maggie had made to Brigid's attempts at conversation.

"The new snow," Brigid sighed now, "makes it look like the whole town is being served up as dessert for a giant. And he wanted it topped with whipping cream."

"Mother," Maggie complained. "Brigid is so annoying sometimes."

It was true that Brigid could be exasperating. She was always comparing one thing to another, and the more fanciful, the better. Maggie thought her sister lived in a dream world. Brigid was just like her twin brother, Aidan, whose freckled nose was always buried in a book.

Maggie gazed out of the window across Hobson Street. The snow-covered homes on her street were much smaller and closer together than those on Jefferson Street. Homes like Beth's.

Maggie didn't envy Beth the advantages of her family's wealth. But she didn't like to feel that Beth, or anyone else on Jefferson Street, would look down on folks of more modest means.

Maggie loved Hobson Street, and she never wanted to leave it. And let anyone try to tell her that she wasn't as good as they were, just because of something so unimportant as money!

Of course, Maggie knew that money was a necessity. It was the reason that her father had had to go west to work with the railway company. His last letter had come from Colorado.

"Sit like a lady," Mrs. Sullivan scolded Maggie cheerfully. "Daisy already knows how to sit properly, and she's only three years old!"

Maggie uncurled her legs from beneath her and turned to look at Daisy, sitting on a stool by the fire. She did indeed look dainty, with her chubby ankles crossed, quietly combing her doll's curls. The doll's hair was the same color as Daisy's–a very golden red, looking more gold than ever in the flickering firelight. She looked sweet enough to eat, and Maggie swooped down on her.

Daisy (which was the Irish nickname for Deirdre) enjoyed the hug, but seemed just as glad when Maggie set her free again. Setting herself back on the stool, Daisy straightened her skirts carefully.

"Daisy," Maggie exclaimed, "you were born to be a duchess."

"Perhaps she *was* born a duchess," said Aidan, looking up from his book. The firelight made his hair look like burnished copper. It was actually a deep auburn. All of the Sullivan children had hair in different shades of red. Daisy's was the lightest and Aidan's the darkest. Maggie's copper, Brigid's carrot, and Kevin's rust were in between.

"Perhaps Daisy was born into the Irish peerage," Aidan suggested. "And the babies were switched by fairies!"

Aidan never went anywhere without a book. And whenever he emerged from between the book's covers, what he had to say usually sounded as though it had come from a story.

"Daisy was *not* switched at birth!" laughed their mother. "And I'll thank you, sir, not to imply that a child with fine airs and graces couldn't have been born into the Sullivan family."

Maggie turned back to the window. She wondered if the new snow had been cleared from the river yet.

Maggie's scowl deepened. She wasn't going skating this afternoon. She told herself that it was because she just didn't feel like skating.

Chapter Two

Buttons And Beaux

After school on Monday, the four friends gathered on the large porch of the schoolhouse. Maggie and Beth were very quiet. This was strange, for they usually did most of the talking.

Hannah tilted her head to one side and looked from Beth to Maggie and back again. Then she asked Ellie, "Shall we walk down to McGuire's store and see if those new buttons have arrived?"

The four recently discovered they each had a button collection. Beth and Hannah kept theirs in large, old candy tins. Ellie had a wooden box and Maggie, a glass jar shaped like a high-buttoned shoe.

Each girl had been saving buttons for years, starting with odd, one-of-a-kind buttons left over from household sewing. But spurred by the fun of a mutual hobby, the four were now actually purchasing buttons for their collections.

11

The friends turned to walk down the school steps together. Ellie and Hannah tried to keep the conversation going.

"Grandma says you all ought to come out to my house to do our baking on Saturday," Ellie added cautiously.

"What shall we bake this week?" Hannah asked.

After a moment of silence, Ellie ventured, "What about spice muffins?"

"Or banana muffins," suggested Hannah. I stopped in at the grocer's this morning to get a packet of tea for Mama, and Mr. Johnson told me that he wouldn't be surprised if he had a bunch of very ripe bananas at a cut price for us on Saturday morning."

They turned in at McGuire's Books and Notions and paused by the door to study a large poster. "AUDITION," it read, "for the Following Parts in the Winter Entertainment of St. Luke's Church." The list called for men and women to sing parts . . . and for a child to sing the part of a "Snow Princess."

The girls all turned to Hannah, who was holding her breath as she stared at the poster. Mrs. McGuire was watching them from behind the candy counter with a smile on her face. "I knew you'd be happy to see that," she said.

"You mean," said Hannah, "you think I should

audition for the Snow Princess?"

"Of course you should!" Mrs. McGuire exclaimed. "You're more than ready. You sing like a bird!"

Hannah had been taking voice lessons with Mrs. McGuire every week all winter long. This was one of the reasons that the girls kept up their "Best Bakers" business on Saturdays. Hannah's share of the proceeds helped pay for her lessons.

"I don't know, Mrs. McGuire," Hannah murmured. "Singing in front of strangers? I don't know if I can do it."

"Hannah," said Mrs. McGuire, "I thought your goal was to become a singer! Didn't you think about the audience?!"

"Well, no," Hannah replied hesitantly. "I guess I didn't."

"This will be an excellent experience for you. And if you find that your dread of singing before an audience is greater than your hope of becoming a singer, then you'll know that a performance career isn't for you."

"Oh! I'm sure it isn't! I mean, I'm sure it is! I mean . . . I'll try, Mrs. McGuire! Will you help me get ready for the audition?"

"Of course," Mrs. McGuire smiled approvingly.

"Now what will it be today? A book, a button, or a bonbon?"

McGuire's was a rather curious store. Before they had married, Mr. McGuire ran the local bookshop. And his future wife had owned a piece-goods store, selling fabric, ribbons, and buttons. After their marriage, the couple rolled the two businesses into one, with the addition of a candy counter. "Because I have a sweet tooth," Mrs. McGuire had told them with a wink.

"We're wondering about that card of rhinestone buttons you told us you were expecting?" Ellie asked Mrs. McGuire politely.

"Here it is," said Mrs. McGuire, crossing to a glass case opposite the candy counter. "There's four on a card."

The girls could see the buttons glittering inside the case as soon as they turned around.

"They're so pretty!" cried Hannah.

"That will be forty cents," Mrs. McGuire said.

At that moment, Hannah caught sight of Mr. Moore, a teacher in the upper grades at school, who was looking at a rack of valentines. She nudged the others, who looked up as he chose a large red and white heart, edged with fabric lace. It was clearly a valentine for a sweetheart.

"Hello, ladies," he said as the upturned faces caught his eye. He spoke casually, but he looked a bit flustered as he moved to the section of books.

"I wonder who Mr. Moore's valentine is," whispered Beth.

"Henry!" Mr. McGuire greeted him heartily. "Hope to see you at the Pre-Emption House this evening!" The Pre-Emption house was one of Oakdale's two hotels. The gentlemen of the town often held political meetings there.

Mrs. McGuire brought the girls' attention back to the rhinestone buttons.

"They're more expensive than most of the buttons you've chosen this winter," Mrs. McGuire cautioned them, as each girl produced a dime.

"We're dividing the card four ways," Ellie explained.

"Besides," swaggered Maggie, glancing at Beth, "money is no object."

Mrs. McGuire looked at Maggie curiously. Maggie looked unconcerned, but the three other girls looked uncomfortable.

Chapter
Three

Stirring Up Memories

The girls met at Ellie's on Saturday morning to bake. Beth brought along the bananas, as she came right by the grocer's store. Normally, Maggie would have walked with Beth, but today they had arrived at Ellie's separately.

The atmosphere felt less strained as they began to work. The Perry kitchen was cozy with the morning sunlight streaming in through the windows, which were hung with blue gingham curtains. Bright red geraniums bloomed in pots along the counter by the window sill. Cleo, Ellie's calico cat, purred on the blue checked cushion of a kitchen chair.

The girls had developed a system for their baking projects. Ellie always prepared the fruit, mashing it into a smooth mixture. Hannah always sifted the flour, soda, salt, and cream of tartar. Beth beat the eggs and oil together, while Maggie greased the muffin tins.

The Best Bakers had purchased several of their own muffin tins so that they could double or triple their recipes. They sold as many as six dozen muffins on a Saturday. By now, they even had regular customers who counted on them. Sometimes they received special requests. Mrs. Martin-Mitchell at Pine Craig Mansion had asked for three dozen scones on several occasions.

Ellie's grandma kept the bakers entertained with a story about the early days of Oakdale, shortly after the Civil War. "You remember," she'd often begin, "Oakdale was out here on the Illinois prairie even before Chicago itself. It was founded in 1830–nearly seventy years ago! Of course, I wasn't born yet myself then ... not quite, anyway!

"After the War Between the States, Ellie's grandfather and I came here with an officer with whom he'd become friendly in the war. And together they founded the quarry.

"Oakdale was a fine town to settle in. It was the first town in DuPage County. Of course, it hasn't always been in DuPage County!" Mrs. Perry laughed.

"What do you mean, Grandma?" asked Ellie. "Surely the town didn't move."

"No, of course not! But the county lines did.

Many times. This area was considered part of the Old
Virginia Colony until 1884. It was later part of
Indiana Territory, then Illinois Territory. After Illinois
became a state, the large counties were carved up into
smaller counties. A lot of it was politics. In fact, it's
still going on."

"I know what you mean!" cried Beth. "I've heard
my father and the other councilmen talking about
Westbrook. They say Westbrook won't give up the
county seat to us, because they had it first."

"That's right," said Grandma Perry. "Westbrook

19

was once the county seat, but when the county lines were redrawn, it was no longer a good choice. Folks need a county seat to be near the center of the county, so everyone can get to it easily. Westbrook is too far north. But they don't want to give it up. Sounds like it's a real battle."

"Tell us about the street names again, Mrs. Perry," suggested Beth.

"Well, Beth, you know that one of the trouble-makers was your own great-grandfather. He died a few years after we came, but I remember him well. It seems that he was one of the earliest settlers to arrive in the town–and one of the folks with the biggest ideas!

"Jefferson Street was just a little dirt road when he came along. It was his idea to make it a wide boulevard with flower beds down the middle–'just like they have in Paris,' he said."

"I wish I'd known Great-Grandpa Dunstable," sighed Beth.

"I bet his favorite color was pink, just like yours," Maggie said under her breath.

"What did you say?" asked Hannah.

"Nothing," said Maggie.

Grandma Perry looked from Maggie to Beth with

worried eyes. "You girls don't seem quite your smiling selves this morning. Is there trouble?"

No one answered. They each pretended to be very busy with their tasks.

The kitchen was quiet for a few moments.

"Friendship is a funny thing," said Grandma Perry at last. "Sometimes you get along so well that you can't imagine ever *not* getting along. But no friendship is perfect. We have to forgive each other for our flaws, or no one would ever have a friend!"

Maggie and Beth exchanged glances.

"Old George Dunstable had his feuds," Grandma Perry continued. "One of them was over the name of one of the major roads. It crossed several lots which he owned, and he wanted to name the street after his wife, Ann. But a friend who owned adjacent land wanted to name the street after *his* wife. And that's why the street names in that part of town change at Jefferson Street. When you are north of Jefferson, Ann Street becomes Victoria Lane!

"And the saddest part of the story is that George Dunstable and Simon Forsythe never did shake hands and forgive each other. Their friendship was lost. Isn't that a pity?"

Once again, no one answered.

CHAPTER FOUR

VALENTINE MYSTERY

Snowflake leaped onto Beth's bed and she awoke to a kiss from a wet nose.

"Happy Valentine's Day, Snowflake!" Beth sang out. But she frowned thoughtfully as she glanced at the red paper bag on her dresser which held the valentines she had made.

She jumped out of bed in a hurry and ran down to breakfast early. "I want to talk to you, Papa," she said quite seriously.

"Yes, Miss Pink. I shall be glad to submit to your interrogation." Mr. Dunstable called Beth "Miss Pink" because it was her favorite color.

"Don't be silly," she said. "This is important. I want to know about the county seat. How are you going to make Westbrook give it up?"

Mr. Dunstable looked startled. "What do you mean?" he asked.

"Well, Grandma Perry said that Oakdale is to be

the new county seat, but Westbrook won't let it. What does that mean?" Beth questioned.

"It was over a year ago that a poll was taken to see where people in this county wanted their county offices. Westbrook had been the county seat for some years, but with the changes in the county lines, it wasn't central. And besides, it wasn't on a railroad line. The ballots were cast, and it came down in favor of Oakdale. The township supervisors even built a new courthouse on Central Park. But why isn't it in use? Westbrook won't give up the county records. So everyone still has to go there to conduct county business. You can see why folks are upset," Mr. Dunstable concluded.

"What is the Town Council going to do about it?" asked Beth.

"We'll see," Mr. Dunstable said, rubbing his chin. "We'll see."

§

Miss Devine always found it difficult to keep the children's attention on their studies on Valentine's Day. This year, it was worse than ever.

The children had constructed a valentine wishing

well, covered with bright red and white paper. The students had "mailed" their valentines in the wishing well as they came in that morning. They couldn't seem to keep their eyes off the well, and they all walked by it to peer inside on their way to and from the blackboard.

At the back of the room, the refreshments for the party had been arranged on a table by Ellie and Polly Sanders. Polly was very shy and quiet. Ellie had a hard time hearing what Polly said, she was so soft-spoken. Ellie had brought in muffins, of course. Her grandmother had made them with cherries and had sprinkled red granulated sugar across the top, in honor of Valentine's Day.

"Polly!" Ellie exclaimed, when she saw Polly's contribution to the table. It was a plate of exquisite cookies. They were all shaped like hearts, but each one was a little different from the others.

"They all came from the same kind of batter," Polly apologized.

"But that doesn't matter!" Ellie said. "They are so beautiful. Each one is a little work of art!"

Some were cut with scalloped edges. They were painted delicately with icing–in looping bands or with arrows. One had a little Cupid painted on it. "My mama did that one," Polly said shyly.

Beth had brought in an unusual valentine that she had received from her uncle. It had been decorated with silver and gold paint. "My uncle is a British officer," she said. "He's stationed in India."

Hannah and Ellie both frowned. They were afraid that Maggie, in her present frame of mind, would think that Beth was bragging. From the sour look on Maggie's face, they were right.

The rest of the class was interested to see Beth's valentine which had come from so far away. And they were even more eager to see what the wishing well held for each of them.

That afternoon, Miss Devine sighed with relief when the time finally came for the party. "All right!" she said. "Daniel O'Leary, come to the front of the room!"

Daniel had been chosen to draw the cards from the wishing well one by one. He would call out the name, and the child it belonged to would come up to claim it.

This process took some time, but the children seemed to delight in the suspense. By the time Daniel reached the bottom of the wishing well, each desk held

a small mound of white and red valentines.

The last card Daniel pulled from the well was the largest of all. It was a red heart, decorated with real fabric lace around the edges. Daniel read the name at the top.

"Why, it's for Miss Devine," he said with some surprise.

26

Beth, Hannah, Maggie, and Ellie exchanged glances. It was the very valentine they had seen Mr. Moore purchasing at McGuire's store! But they would keep his secret. They didn't say a word to anyone else.

Miss Devine blushed a deep pink. She put the valentine inside her desk. Then she got up to walk around the room and admire the children's valentines.

"This is a lovely one, Ellie!" she said, looking at a valentine that had been decorated with buttons.

"Maggie made it," responded Ellie. "I think she meant us to take the buttons off for our collections— but the valentine is too pretty to take apart!"

Miss Devine stopped to look at the button valentine on Hannah's desk, too. But when she looked over at Beth, Beth was looking down and her face was red.

"Didn't Maggie make one for Beth?" Miss Devine whispered to Hannah.

"No," answered Hannah. "And Beth didn't give one to Maggie, either. They're not getting along very well."

Miss Devine gave Hannah's hand an encouraging squeeze. But she looked troubled as she continued down the aisle.

CHAPTER FIVE

PUTTING TWO AND TWO TOGETHER

The next Saturday, all four girls met at the river to skate. It was the first time they had been back to the river together since the quarrel had begun.

When they tired of skating, the girls walked down the gently sloping bank to a bench by the river. They began to take off their skates. Maggie was using her brother's, and Beth knew better than to say anything about her extra pair sitting at home.

"Are you getting excited about the Winter Entertainment, Hannah?" Beth asked instead. Hannah had indeed been given the part of the Snow Princess. Her audition had gone beautifully, but she was very modest about it.

"Yes," responded Hannah. "And did I tell you that

they wanted two little snowflakes? My little sister Jennie and Maggie's sister Daisy are nearly the same age. Jennie just turned four. They're going to be the snowflakes!"

The sun was low and the western sky was streaked with navy blue and purple ribbons. The world had begun to take on a lavender hue. The snowy riverbank glowed blue.

A pair of skaters appeared on the bank out to the west, farther from town. Their figures looked very black, skating arm in arm, against the sunset sky. The four girls watched them in silence. "It looks like a painting," Ellie commented solemnly.

The couple turned back before they reached the part of the river where the girls had been skating. The river hadn't been kept as clear of snow to the west, but the couple didn't seem to mind the bumps and ridges in the ice. They were talking quietly, and the woman laughed softly.

"Miss Devine!" the four girls whispered together.

"And that's Mr. Moore she's with," Maggie pointed out.

They were all thinking of the last valentine to come out of the wishing well.

CHAPTER
SIX

BUMPS & BRUISES

The next week, three storms hit the Illinois prairie. The snow piled up to the window ledges. There had been no school. But after several days of bright, sunny weather, Hannah's father brought her into town on the wagon. They stopped at the little red house by the quarry for Ellie.

The wind stung their faces as the wagon sped along on its winter runners, but Mr. Olson enjoyed the cold weather. "This is the first time I've had the runners on the wagon in three years. Been so mild and so little snow. We're sure making up for it this winter, aren't we?"

"We've had nearly two feet of new snow," Ellie added.

"I wonder if the river will have been cleared for skating," mused Hannah.

"Those high-school boys don't seem to have anything better to do with their time!" Mr. Olson remarked. "I imagine they'll have the river clear by next week."

As the wagon passed McGuire's, Hannah and Ellie caught sight of Maggie, just coming out the door with a green-and-white-striped stick of peppermint in her mouth.

"Hi!" they called. "Come along, Beth's expecting us." Mr. Olson stopped the wagon so Maggie could climb in. She was bubbling with excitement.

"I was down at the river watching the boys work on the snow. They're shoveling up a storm. All that snow flying through the air makes quite a sight!"

Mr. Olson dropped the girls off at Beth's house on Jefferson Street. "I'll be back this afternoon," he said as he drove off.

Agnes greeted them at the door. They found Beth sitting at the foot of the staircase, tossing hats at a massive oak rack. A pile of hats, belonging to her and to her father, lay on the floor at the bottom.

"What's the score?" asked Ellie.

"Nine to three. The hat rack's winning," Beth replied with a grin.

At that moment, a loud voice from Mr.

Dunstable's study boomed out. "If we have to use force, so be it!"

"That's Judge Cody," Beth said. "He gets kind of loud."

"What are they talking about?" Hannah asked.

"Westbrook, I think," Beth answered.

"What does he mean by 'force'?"

"I can't imagine." Beth furrowed her brow. "Politics is beyond me."

"What shall we do today?" asked Ellie. "Hannah's father says there won't be any skating until next week. Too much snow."

"Well," said Beth, "There's a toboggan out in the carriage house. I'll ask Agnes to help us get it down, it's pretty heavy."

Agnes grumbled, but she put on her coat and boots and tramped out to the carriage house with them. She got out the ladder and lowered the toboggan into the arms of the waiting girls.

"Where shall we go?" Hannah asked.

"Why don't you go down to Pine Craig and ask Mrs. Martin-Mitchell if you might coast down her hill?" Agnes suggested. "It's good and steep. But you be sure to stop and ask permission of Mrs. Martin-Mitchell first!"

"Pine Craig it is!" smiled Beth.

Agnes waved them off as Maggie and Beth pulled the toboggan down Jefferson Street. As they approached Pine Craig, they could see that other children had had the same idea.

"Do you suppose we really need to ask permission?" asked Maggie, looking at the other sleds and toboggans coasting down the hill. "She obviously doesn't mind if children use her hill."

Ellie pushed down her yellow muffler to scratch her chin. "Agnes said we ought to."

The four girls approached the large brick mansion. "I always think it's a little spooky," whispered Hannah. "Look at the roof."

The roof had a little iron gate going around it.

"That's called a mansard roof," said Beth. "It's very fashionable. I think it's a beautiful house."

"It is beautiful," said Hannah. "But I still think it's a little spooky."

Beth put on her best manners as she turned the knob that rang a little bell.

Mrs. Martin-Mitchell opened the door herself, as usual. Though, Beth realized, she must have several maids who could do it for her.

"Good morning!" she said to the girls. "What

treats do you have for me this time? Muffins or scones?"

"Oh, we didn't bake today," apologized Beth. "But we'll be sure to stop here first, the next time we do. Today we're here to ask a favor."

Mrs. Martin-Mitchell looked beyond to their toboggan on the lawn. "Of course," she said. "You've come to coast. You are most welcome. As you can see, our hill is a popular spot. The children know that they are welcome. But I must say, it's rather pleasant to have someone stop and ask for permission!"

The four girls thanked her and waved merrily as they returned to the toboggan.

They pulled it around to the back of the house, where the lawn spread out beneath several dozen beautiful black-walnut trees. Beyond the trees, the lawn dropped into a sudden hill. Children were calling to each other happily as they went zipping down, then trudged back up, pulling sleds and toboggans behind them.

"It looks kind of crowded," worried Ellie. "Do you think we ought to come back another day?"

"But today is perfect for coasting!" exclaimed Maggie. "We'll be careful."

The hill was steep, and the foursome had some trouble getting the toboggan over to the knoll. This time, instead of them pulling it, it almost pulled them. The toboggan seemed very eager to coast down that hill. The girls were less eager, except for Maggie.

With misgivings, they climbed into the toboggan– Beth in front, followed by Ellie and Hannah. Maggie planned to hop on after giving them a push.

At that moment, their classmate, Murgatroyd Forsythe, called out to them with a jeer from the front of a large toboggan as it whizzed past, coming down from the hill just behind them.

"Come on!" shouted Maggie. "Let's catch him!" She grabbed Hannah's shoulders and gave the toboggan a shove, jumping onto the back at the last second. The cold wind whistled into their faces, while the bright sun on the snow nearly blinded them.

Beth steered straight down the slope.

Murg's long toboggan held eight boys. With their added weight, they hadn't picked up the speed which the girls were rapidly acquiring.

"Where's the brake?" shouted Ellie into the wind.

"We're catching them!" Maggie shouted back gleefully, not hearing Ellie.

The girls were indeed passing the boys as they

hurdled down the hill. The boys appeared to be listing to one side, which slowed them even further.

Halfway down, Maggie looked back to see why Murg's toboggan was tipping. "Yikes!" she cried.

Murg had hollered for the boys in the back of his toboggan to roll off, so that he could catch the girls. And not only was his toboggan now speeding towards them at an alarming rate, but he was pulling to the right, steering straight across their path.

"Watch out!" shrieked Hannah. "Beth, pull the lines to the right! Pull, Beth, pull!"

Beth pulled right–looking up to see a huge oak tree in front of her. That was the last thing she saw, before her eyes were filled with a blaze of twinkling stars.

The impact was softened by a deep snowdrift at the foot of the tree, but Beth had still received a good knock on her head. The other girls had tumbled out of the toboggan unhurt, rolling into the soft snow.

Murg roared down the hill with a frightened look on his face.

CHAPTER SEVEN

HOT CHOCOLATE IN
AN OCTAGON

"What's your name?" demanded Maggie. She had heard her father ask this question of a man who'd been knocked unconscious.

Beth saw the faces of her friends as the stars began to clear from before her eyes.

"What do you mean, 'What's my name?'" retorted Beth. "Do you think I've forgotten who I am?"

"She's just trying to make sure you're all right, Beth!" soothed Ellie.

They moved a white-faced Beth carefully onto the toboggan and pulled her slowly back up to Pine Craig. It was the closest house, and they felt that they rather knew Mrs. Martin-Mitchell now.

This time a maid in a frilled white apron opened the front door. "What's this?" she asked in concern. "I'll call the mistress."

Mrs. Martin-Mitchell came out of her conservatory with a rustle of satin skirts. And how relieved the girls were to see, coming behind, none other than their own Miss Devine!

"Well, I needn't ask what the trouble is," Miss Devine said. "There's a goose egg coming up on Beth's forehead that tells the story!"

"Bring her into the Octagon and set her down on the settee."

Ellie and Hannah supported Beth on either side. Maggie came behind, alternately wringing her hands and making fists.

Beth sat back on the little couch with a sigh. "That's better. Walking up the steps hurt my head."

After the maid arrived with an ice bag, Mrs. Martin-Mitchell sent for a tray of hot chocolate. "It'll help everybody settle down," she said reassuringly.

The girls looked around the conservatory with pleasure. It was built off the rear of the house, with large doors that could be opened out to the snow-covered garden. It looked more like a beautiful hothouse rather than any of the Oakdale parlors they had visited.

Blooming plants grew everywhere–in pots and in trays. Flowering vines climbed a little white trellis. The walls were of glass and there were no drapes– only delicate lace balloon shades looping across each section of glass wall.

Most unusual was the shape of the room. Including the wall which joined it to the back of the house, the room had eight walls!

"I suddenly realized why you call your conservatory the 'Octagon'!" Ellie exclaimed.

"I was thinking the same thing," said Hannah. "What a lovely room!"

"Gardening is my favorite hobby," Mrs. Martin-Mitchell explained. "And since I can't do it outdoors in winter, I do it indoors! My husband was an architect, and he designed it for me. With these glass walls, the room is bright enough to grow nearly anything—even in winter."

The color had returned to Beth's cheeks, and she looked up expectantly as a tray of hot chocolate and cakes was brought in.

"This is a real treat!" Beth exclaimed. "It was worth getting my head knocked!"

"I guess she's feeling better," Miss Devine smiled.

"Such gorgeous little cakes!" Beth exclaimed.

"What are they called, Mrs. Martin-Mitchell?" asked Ellie, accepting a white iced cake with a pink flower on top. The cake wasn't

much bigger than a small grape.

"They're petits fours," Mrs. Martin-Mitchell said. "That's fondant icing on them. Very sugary and sweet. But not as satisfying as the delicious muffins I buy from some local bakers!"

The girls smiled at each other. They helped themselves to generous spoonfuls of whipped cream.

Mrs. Martin-Mitchell sprinkled cinnamon over the top of her cup. Maggie wanted to try it, too. "Ummm!" she said. "Could we try baking cinnamon-chocolate muffins?"

When the petits fours had disappeared and the hot chocolate was gone, the maid came for the tray and Miss Devine rose.

"I must go. Look at the time!" she said, glancing out the glass walls at the red and gold spreading in the western sky. "I have to meet . . . that is, I have to go! We'll send a message over to your father to let him know what happened, Beth. I imagine he'll want to come for you in the carriage."

"What were you doing here, Miss Devine? If you don't mind my asking," Maggie added hastily.

"Not at all, Maggie. I come here fairly often.

Mrs. Martin-Mitchell is my aunt," Miss Devine said, smiling.

"We were looking at fashion sheets today," Mrs. Martin-Mitchell added. Miss Devine was hastily gathering together loose pages showing elaborate gowns.

Before long Mr. Dunstable came to drive the girls home. He insisted on carrying Beth out in his arms. "Like a baby," she protested.

Snug under carriage robes, the four looked at each other. "What an adventure!" Ellie sighed.

"I don't know if it was worth a bump on the noggin," said Hannah, "but hot chocolate in the Octagon was quite an experience! Say, girls, did any of you get a look at those drawings Miss Devine had?"

"Yes!" they responded in unison, eyes widened. They looked at each other. All the sheets had shown designs that looked like . . . bridal gowns!

CHAPTER EIGHT

MIDNIGHT ADVENTURE

Beth arrived at school the next morning in a great flurry, with flushed cheeks and flashing eyes.

"Heavens, Beth!" Ellie cried. "Are you well?"

"I'm fine, but wait 'til you hear what I know!"

"Tell us!" exclaimed Hannah.

"Not now. It will have to wait until we can talk in private. But you have to know now that we're going to bake at my house tomorrow morning. And you can all spend the night tonight with me. You have to!"

"What are you talking about?" demanded Ellie.

"It's that bump on the head," murmured Maggie.

The girls hadn't noticed that Murg Forsythe had been listening curiously. But Beth said no more and Miss Devine began the school day.

Beth wouldn't say a word about her secret until recess began and she had drawn the girls around to the back of the schoolhouse.

"You won't believe it," she said. "But we're going to be part of history tonight."

"What?" Ellie and Hannah cried together.

"It's that bump on her head," Maggie repeated.

"It's not the bump. It's what I overheard this morning. Papa was in his study with Judge Cody and some of the other council members. I didn't mean to eavesdrop, but their voices came right through the wall."

"What were they talking about?" Ellie asked.

"They were going over the final details of 'the plan,' " Beth told them mysteriously.

"What plan?" Maggie asked impatiently. "Will you get to the bottom of it?"

"The plan to steal the county records from Westbrook. In the middle of the night. Tonight. And we're going, too!"

"Steal records?" Ellie's eyes widened in surprise.

"Well, not really *steal*," Beth explained. " The records belong to Oakdale. You remember Grandma Perry telling us that Oakdale was the new county seat, but Westbrook wouldn't give us the records? Well, the Town Council plans to *take* them."

"And your father said we could go along?" asked Hannah.

"Of course not! I didn't ask him. But we're
going. They're leaving from the Pre-Emption
House at midnight. Tonight. They've got the
whole thing planned. Every detail. Now we have
to make our own plan. We'll work it out at my
house after school."

What the girls didn't know was that they had
been the victim of an eavesdropper themselves.
Murg had had to stay in the classroom to complete
yesterday's unfinished homework. Restless, he had
gone to the windows to look for his friends.
Finding that the four girls had unluckily placed
themselves directly below, he opened the window
and heard the whole story.

But what Murg didn't know was that *he* had
been observed himself. Ben Tarken had brought
up a fresh bucket of water to the classroom at
recess, and seeing Murg absorbed at the window,
entered on tiptoe. He couldn't hear everything that
was being said below, but one phrase floated
through the glass clearly. "The Pre-Emption
House at midnight–tonight." And Ben had seen
Murg's lips curl in a mischievous grin.

After school, the girls enlisted Polly's help to

carry messages to Ellie's grandmother and to Hannah's family at Cherry Hill Farm to let them know that the girls were spending the night at Beth's house. Aidan was sent to tell Maggie's mother.

The girls hurried to Beth's house and rushed up the stairs. Beth closed her bedroom door behind them and turned the key in the lock. The four girls put their heads together to discuss their own "plan" to go along on the raid of the Westbrook courthouse.

By nightfall, word had come that the three girls had permission to spend the night with Beth. They had a delicious pot-roast dinner with Aunt Mary. Mr. Dunstable had been detained on business, Agnes told them. The girls gave each other knowing looks. "Business indeed!"

Ellie and Hannah had some reservations about joining in the business themselves, but it was an adventure they could not resist. And it wasn't as though they–or the Town Council–would be breaking any laws. Or would they?

Hannah thought they should try to take a catnap in the evening, but they were all too excited to sleep.

They had assembled an assortment of black and dark-colored hats, scarves, gloves, and cloaks. They didn't want to be seen!

Snowflake almost foiled them as they slipped out the bedroom door at half-past eleven, but Beth shushed him sternly after his first yap, and he hid himself under the bed.

"I'd kind of like to join him," Ellie whispered.

"Me, too!" Hannah whispered back. "I'm scared."

"Shh!" hissed Beth.

The girls eased down the front stairs, across the front hall, and out the back door.

There wasn't much moonlight, and they were glad of it. "That was part of the plan, too," said Beth. "Choosing a dark night."

Single file, in their dark clothing, they padded softly over to Main Street. "I feel like we're going to the Boston Tea Party," giggled Ellie.

"But we're not dressed like Indians," Hannah laughed.

"Shh!" cautioned Beth again.

It was only a few blocks to the Pre-Emption House, where several wagons waited out front. Four men stood talking quietly nearby. The girls inched along the street until they were directly across from the hotel.

They could see into the backs of the wagons, which were filled with empty crates and barrels. Suddenly, a beam of light revealed that someone was coming out of the Pre-Emption House. The four men turned towards the door, and the girls seized the chance to slip into the nearest wagon.

They kneeled behind some barrels at the back of the wagon and waited, holding their breath until they were sure that no one had spotted them. The men continued talking quietly.

But someone *had* seen them! Murg Forsythe raised himself up silently from behind a watering trough across the street. He chuckled softly and settled himself back down to wait a little longer.

Soon more men began coming out of the Pre-Emption House. Beth heard her father's voice. Other men arrived on foot and on horseback. At midnight, they moved out.

As their wagon got underway, the girls peeped over the side. They gasped as they saw Murg Forsythe standing at the edge of the street. But just as he opened his mouth to cry out and reveal the presence of the girls, he received a violent push

from a figure that had rocketed out from behind a
rain barrel. As the wagon passed, the girls caught
sight of Murg flying headfirst into a snowbank.
Ben Tarken stood on the wooden sidewalk, waving
with a wide grin.

CHAPTER NINE

THE SNOW PRINCESS

The next day, Oakdale was buzzing with the news that it was now truly the county seat, records and all. (Westbrook was no doubt buzzing, too.)

The girls told their story over and over. There were many visitors to the Dunstable house, and all wanted to hear about their bird's-eye view of the seizure of the records. They never got around to their Saturday baking that day.

The foursome had been discovered–but not until the wagons had completed their mission and were back in Oakdale at the new courthouse, unloading their rightful property.

Mr. Dunstable had been appalled to find the girls in the wagon, and he had spoken to them severely back at the house. It had been very foolish of them. But he supposed that all was well that ended well. And they certainly had witnessed a historic event. It would be something to tell their grandchildren about someday.

It had been very exciting, the girls recalled. As the

wagons slipped quietly through town, they had been joined by other town members, until there were forty men. They had proceeded in silence to Westbrook, where they backed the wagons up to the rear windows of the old courthouse.

A sympathetic county employee, formerly of Oakdale, had agreed to leave one of the windows unlocked. The men climbed in quietly and lugged out the record books and papers to the crates in the wagons. All the court papers, along with the birth, death, marriage, and property records of the county, were loaded in. And a couple of hours later, Oakdale was the new county seat!

Rumors and stories flew wildly around town. One said that the four girls had been the ones to slip through the window and carry out the record books. (It wasn't true.) Another said that the sweetheart of the man who had left the window unlocked had left him forever because of his "treachery" to Westbrook.

It was lunchtime before Hannah remembered the Winter Entertainment. "It's tonight!" she cried. "I promised Mrs. McGuire I would rehearse my song with her this afternoon!"

Hannah set off for the McGuires' while Ellie and Maggie headed home. They would all see each other that evening with their families for the Winter Entertainment.

Hannah was stopped three times on her way to the McGuires' house on Eagle Street. People wanted to ask questions about last night. But Hannah now had her mind on her performance.

Her Snow Princess costume hung in Mrs. McGuire's parlor. It was all in white, with a silvery overskirt atop layers of tulle. It made Hannah feel like a ballerina when she tried it on. She was to wear a crown of shimmering snowflakes and carry a wand hung with white and silver ribbons.

Hannah's stomach was starting to feel fluttery. "I'm glad that the council chose last night to seize the county records," Hannah told Mrs. McGuire. "People will still be too excited about it tonight to pay much attention to the performance!"

Hannah was right about the excitement continuing to ride high. But she was wrong about the town not paying attention to the Snow Princess.

On the whole, the Winter Entertainment was a bit boring. Mr. Johnson, the grocer who sold the girls fruit for their muffins, surprised everyone by singing a tenor aria called "La Donna e Mobile."

"Did you know that Mr. Johnson could sing?" Beth

whispered to her father.

"Wonders never cease," he whispered back.

Even lovers of classical music seemed to appreciate the change when the time came for the Snow Princess piece.

The curtain on the small stage opened slowly. Glittery snowflakes had been pinned to the backdrop. When the tinkling music began, Hannah came onto the stage with a little spin, slow and graceful.

She stopped in the center and began to sing. If she was nervous, she didn't look it ... or sound it. At the chorus, the little snowflakes, Daisy Sullivan and Jennie Olson, twirled out onto the stage. They carried little white baskets from which they tossed handfuls of tissue-paper snowflakes. It was very effective, until Jennie tripped and dropped her basket at the end of the song! The audience cheered as Hannah stooped down to retrieve the basket and gave it back to the "snowflake."

Ellie and her grandmother were sitting near the front, close to the Sullivan and Olson families. Ellie, Maggie, and Beth felt as proud of Hannah as all her brothers and sisters did.

Under the cover of applause, Hannah's older

sister Rachel, who also sang, whispered that Hannah ought to have prepared an encore. For the Snow Princess and her court of snowflakes had to come out for three bows.

When the show was over and the Olsons were back on the farm, Hannah snuggled into bed with a sigh. Beside her on the pillow was a little bouquet of violets which had been shyly given to her by Ben after the show.

It had been a very exciting twenty-four hours. And Hannah was rather glad that the excitement was over. At least, she thought it was!

CHAPTER TEN

BLIZZARD ON THE FARM

Everyone expected life to return to normal after the excitement of the weekend, but there were still some surprises in store.

The girls' first hint that something was afoot came Wednesday morning before school. The girls arrived together early and found Mr. Moore standing beside Miss Devine. "Henry–what if I have to choose?" she asked him.

"Don't worry," he said, patting her hand. "It will all be settled tomorrow night."

Mr. Moore turned to leave and greeted the girls cheerfully. But they could see that Miss Devine had been crying.

"What's tomorrow night?" whispered Beth. The girls shrugged their shoulders.

On Friday morning at breakfast, Mr. Dunstable grinned at Beth in a particularly teasing way. "I know a secret," he said.

"Well?" asked Beth.

"I can't say," he responded.

Beth wouldn't give him the satisfaction of asking again, so she was forced to head off to school thoroughly mystified.

The mystery seemed to continue at school, for Miss Devine was positively beaming, and a beautiful bouquet of white roses stood on her desk. The girls looked at each other with raised eyebrows.

They were glad when Miss Devine called the class to order. Surely she would explain. But she began by confusing them further.

"I have some bad news for you," she said, strangely enough with a serene smile. "Miss Devine will not be your teacher for much longer."

The class stared at her in dismay. Everyone loved Miss Devine.

"The name of your new teacher will be Mrs. Moore."

The pupils sat in stunned silence for a few moments. Beth was the first one to laugh out loud. "You're getting married!" she cried.

Then Miss Devine explained the whole story. Mr. Moore had asked her to be his wife the previous fall. But she hadn't wanted to say yes, because she loved to teach. And when a teacher got married, she lost her job. No school district would hire a married woman.

"I thought I would have to choose between Mr. Moore and my job. That would have been a terrible choice, because they are both very important to me.

"Mr. Moore and I went to the school board meeting on Thursday evening. Some of the Town Council members had come to speak in our favor. We explained the situation, and we were able to convince the school board that there is no reason a woman shouldn't be married and have a job, too."

"So you'll all be invited to a wedding this spring!" she finished with a radiant smile. The children clapped their hands, laughing and cheering.

§

That Saturday, the girls planned to do their baking at Hannah's farm. They hadn't made muffins in several weeks.

Maggie and Beth stopped to call for Ellie. "It looks like a real storm is coming," warned Grandma Perry. "The air has that feel to it."

"I guess it was a good thing we were invited to spend the night," commented Beth.

Snow had begun to fall in fat flakes by the time the girls reached the farm. They decided to do a small baking, just for their families.

Hannah's sister Rachel and her husband, Matthew, had come from their neighboring farm. Hannah was going to give a repeat performance of the Snow Princess song after dinner.

The girls spent the afternoon engaged in a snowman-making contest. The snow was just right for rolling–thick and deep, just wet enough to pack.

Hannah's twelve-year-old brother, Jason, had challenged them. His snowman was of massive proportions. He rolled his first ball until it was nearly as tall as Hannah. The second ball was as tall as Jennie. He had to call his grown-up brothers Joshua and Aaron out to help lift the second ball onto the first, and the third onto the second. He got a ladder from the barn to put an old hat on the top. He didn't worry about a face, but he found two gnarled sticks to make rather frightening arms.

Beth's snowlady was much smaller, but she paid close attention to detail. She used small twigs to make eyelashes above the button eyes.

Maggie's snowman made everyone laugh. She had used an old mop on top for snowman hair. A long carrot nose stuck out from under the mop.

Hannah and Ellie had worked together to make a sculpted snow-mermaid sitting on a large rock. They kept a bucket of warm water nearby and used wet cloths to mold the snow.

Maggie came to admire Beth's elegant snowlady. "I never told you, Beth," Maggie began. "I feel just terrible about that day at Pine Craig. It was my fault that you hit your head. And you never even blamed me."

"That's all right, Maggie. It wasn't your fault. And I'm sorry about the skates. I didn't stop to think about how it might make you feel."

"Now we have just one problem. How are we going to teach that Murg Forsythe a lesson?!" Maggie asked.

Hannah and Ellie saw Maggie and Beth laughing together. "Things have been peaceful for quite some time. I guess we're learning to get along, despite our differences," Ellie remarked happily.

Hannah's little sister Jennie came out with Rachel and her husband, plus Joshua and Aaron, for the judging. But they couldn't agree on the winner. They voted to award first place to each entry.

After dinner, Hannah sang her Snow Princess song, accompanied by Rachel on the organ. The family played games in the parlor and talked about the winter's exciting events. Rachel knew Miss Devine and was looking forward to attending the wedding.

"There's just one problem," Rachel said. "Do you think she would be willing to send one more invitation?"

"What do you mean?" asked Hannah.

"Well, there is one more person who will want to come, if he or she arrives in time, that is."

Hannah stared at Rachel with wide eyes. "Do you mean ...?"

"That's right," said Matthew. "There's going to be an addition to the family."

"It'll be wonderful to be a grandmother," sighed Mrs. Olson, "but kind of strange all the same."

"Rachel's having a baby?!" Beth shouted.

"And in time for the wedding?" asked Maggie.

"Will it be a boy or a girl?" Ellie wondered.

"It's going to be a very exciting spring," Hannah

breathed, collapsing on the sofa behind her. "A baby and a wedding! I can't believe it!"

"Don't worry, Hannah," said Beth, patting her shoulder. "We'll all be right here beside you!"

"You bet," said Maggie. "That's what friends are for."